# LAWFULLY HEROIC

## THE LAWKEEPERS

JENNA BRANDT

## COPYRIGHT

This is a work of fiction. Names, characters, organizations, places, events and incidents are either products of the author's imagination or are used fictitiously. Locale and public names are sometimes used for atmospheric purposes. Any resemblance to actual persons, living or dead, actual events, or actual locations is purely coincidental. All rights reserved.

Visit her on Social Media:

www.JennaBrandt.com
www.facebook.com/JennaBrandtAuthor
Jenna Brandt's Reader Group
hwww.twitter.com/JennaDBrandt
http://www.instagram.com/Jennnathewriter

## Taking Love and Law Seriously

Adam Reynolds has earned a solid reputation as a K9 handler for the Army. He and his partner, Valor, have become experts in searching for bombs, so when he is offered the chance to train at the elite, Disaster City Search and Rescue facility, he jumps at the chance. What he doesn't expect is to fall for one of the female instructors.

Clara Burnette is a decorated K9 instructor at Disaster City Search and Rescue. As a woman in a mostly male-dominated profession, she knows it's never a good idea to get involved with a fellow cop. The problem is, she can't seem to avoid the attraction brewing between her and new recruit, Officer Reynolds.

Can Adam convince Clara to take a chance on him? What will happen when Adam is summoned back to his previous post? And can these two devoted K9 handlers find a way to be together despite everything that keeps getting in the way?

The Lawkeepers is a multi-author series alternating between historical westerns and contemporary westerns featuring law enforcement heroes that span multiple agencies and generations. Join bestselling authors Jenna Brandt, Lorana Hoopes and many others as they weave captivating, sweet and inspirational stories of romance and suspense between the lawkeepers - and the women who love them.

The Lawkeepers is a world like no other; a world where lawkeepers and heroes are honored with unforgettable stories, characters, and love.

** Note: Each book in The Lawkeepers series is a standalone book, in a mini-series, and you can read them in any order.

# ONE

Adam Reynolds ran his hand through his brown hair with frustration. He wasn't sure how many more days he could take of his monotonous routine. He loved working with his K9 partner, Valor, but hated the endless row of cars they inspected daily at the Clear Mountain Army base.

"What's wrong? Are you dreaming of searching terrorists' strongholds for bombs again? You know you have to do years—not months—of posts like this before you ever get to do that," said Greg Walters, the other soldier assigned to the gate. "You should get used to this."

Adam knew Greg was right, but it didn't make him feel any better about the situation. The whole reason he renewed his contract was so that he could cross-train into a position as a K9 handler and go back overseas to detect IEDs. He wanted to stop the type of improvised bombs that killed his squad when he was stationed in Afghanistan. Working at the gate, he felt like he was spinning his wheels as much as the cars that continued to pass by.

A blue Honda Civic pulled up to the gate, and Greg checked the ID of the driver and passengers. Adam moved forward with Valor beside him, leading the German shepherd around the exterior of the car. He let his partner sniff every spot the expertly trained K9 deemed important. Once Valor came back to Adam's side signaling there was nothing to worry about, Adam waved the car through so it could enter the base. Same thing every time. Though he was glad there were no bombs coming onto the base, he wished he could be working an active hot zone.

"Want to go out with us after our shift?" Greg inquired while they waited for the next car to arrive. "We're heading over to The Lucky Penny to grab a couple of beers."

Adam averted his hazel eyes, knowing the other soldier wasn't going to like his answer. "Sorry, I can't; I have plans tonight."

"Let me guess, you have some sort of boring church thing again," Greg said with a roll of his eyes. "You seem to be going to those all the time."

"How about I go out with you guys next time?" Adam suggested, purposely avoiding talking about the activity the other soldier suspected. He didn't like the fact Greg made him feel bad about his plans. He also didn't want to get into a debate, or be forced to defend his choice to attend a men's hang-out started by some guys from Clear Mountain Assembly. It wasn't as stuffy as the other man made it sound. Sometimes they watched sporting events, other times they played cards, but mostly, it was just nice to have some friends that viewed life the same way he did. In the military, he never had that. All the guys ever wanted to do was chase girls and party at bars, neither of which really appealed to Adam.

"Sure, whatever, Adam, I'm not going to hold my breath. You always say you'll go out with us next time, but you never do."

The rest of the afternoon ambled by with more cars passing by without anything out of the ordinary. By the end, Adam was glad to be done with work and ready to have some fun with his friends.

Adam arrived at the rambling farmhouse on the

outskirts of town. He parked his truck, got Valor out of the passenger seat, and made his way up the steps. He knocked on the door, and a few minutes later, it swung open to reveal Officer Aiden O'Connell on the other side, one of the best K9 handlers he'd ever met. "Good to see you, Adam. Come on in. Everyone's waiting in the living room."

Adam made his way inside. The usual guys were there, including several of the Clear Mountain Police Search and Rescue team. Valor waited for Adam to give him the cue it was okay to take off and join Cooper and Harley, Aiden and Zach Turner's K9 partners. Once Adam released him from his leash, he took off running to the edge of the kitchen. He immediately started playing with one of the extra chew toys.

"Come take a seat. The game's about to start," Zach said, gesturing to a seat on the couch. "The pizza should be here in a few minutes."

Adam took the offered spot next to Liam Davis, a local business owner who ran a sleigh-ride company at Clear Mountain Resort. He was engaged to a Clear Mountain Police Detective and set to marry her in a few months.

"How was your day? As eventful as these two

who ended up using their K9 partners to track down a missing kid?" Liam asked with curiosity.

Adam shook his head. "No, just the same old, same old, for me. Valor and I spent our time checking out cars before they passed through the base gate."

"Hey, don't knock it. I would give anything to do what all of you do. I keep waiting for the Captain to add a third K9 position to the department, but he hasn't done it," said Ted Hendricks, another Clear Mountain Search and Rescue officer.

"Ted, your job is just as important as ours," Aiden corrected. "We're a team; don't ever forget that."

"I know that. I've just always wanted to be a K9 handler. Sometimes I think about applying to other departments, but now that I'm in a committed relationship with Deanna, I don't think I could leave her like that."

"Please don't," Zach jokingly begged with a wink. "We don't want our head dispatcher to end up mad because of it. She'd take it out on all of us."

"Okay everyone, the game's about to start," Connor Bishop, the head of the Clear Mountain SWAT team, said as he waved at all of them to be quiet. "I want to see the Broncos sweep the division."

The men settled in around the flat screen TV just as the kickoff took place. Adam enjoyed the rest of the evening with his friends, rooting for their native team and eating lots of junk food. He headed home knowing he was ready to fall fast asleep when his head hit the pillow. What he didn't expect was to find an invitation in his mailbox. It was offering Adam and Valor a chance to join the batch of new recruits for the training program at the elite Disaster City Search and Rescue Academy in Texas.

He'd sent in the application on a whim, never thinking that they would actually want him, let alone that his commanding officer would approve it. Despite the unlikelihood of it actually happening, he held it in his hands. It was physical proof that dreams really could come true. He knew he could finish this training at the top of his class. When he did just that, the Army would have to grant him a post of his choosing. This was the ticket he needed to get back overseas where he belonged.

## TWO

Clara Burnette was happy to have a weekend to herself before the new batch of recruits showed up at the academy for training. The last group had been filled with a lot of newbies who needed extra help, which she was happy to give, but it proved exhausting.

"Can I get you another cucumber water, Miss Burnette?" the hostess at the spa asked as Clara let the masseuse work his magic on her sore legs and feet.

It was rough standing on her feet for hours on end. She wasn't as young as she once was. Approaching her mid-thirties, it was getting harder every year to keep up with the demands of the job. She loved it too much, though, to give it up. It just meant she needed to sneak away more often for her secret spa visits. They had to be secret, too, because her fellow male instructors would never let her live it down if they found out. She always had to be mindful of how they viewed her choices. They would definitely chalk this up to her being dainty, and she wasn't about to let that happen. She'd worked too hard to establish herself as just as capable as her male counterparts.

"No, thanks, Trina. I'm fine for now."

"If you need anything else, just have Henry let me know."

Henry was great at working out the knots in Clara's muscles. She'd gone through several masseuses before finding him. She heard the clicking of the door, letting her know that they were alone again.

"You know, I have this exceptional product, Tiger Balm, that would be great for you to use on any spots giving you a problem between visits."

"Thanks, Henry. I'll take you up on that. Anything to help me get through my long workdays will be much appreciated."

"You know what else helps with that, a cocktail with a friendly face afterward. We should go out sometime."

Clara stiffened, not liking the sound of the invitation. Henry had been flirting heavier and heavier every time she came in for a massage. She'd managed to rebuff him each time since she didn't have time to date. If he wasn't such a great masseuse, she would have stopped coming a long time ago. "Thanks for the offer, Henry, but I'm really busy with work. I can barely get away to get a massage once a month, let alone get enough time to go out."

"You know, all work and no play makes for a very dull life. You should have some fun once in a while, Clara."

"Maybe when I retire," she teased back, trying to deflect his advances. Her phone buzzed, causing her to reach over to the counter and grab it.

"This is a cell phone-free environment. You don't need any stress while you're relaxing," Henry chastised.

"I know, but it could be work." She brushed away her black hair that had fallen into her face. She swiped the line on her phone to unlock it, then squinted her brown eyes to read the words in the dark. Great, it was work. They were getting called out to go inspect a movie theater in Wilmont that received a bomb threat. When small towns nearby didn't have bomb squads of their own, they turned to the Disaster City Search and Rescue Academy to send out a team. The academy didn't have any trainees to send since they were between classes. This meant the instructors would have to go on their own instead, and on her day off, too.

Clara let out a heavy sigh. "I have to go, Henry."

"Another bomb threat?"

She sat up and nodded, as she held the sheet over her. "What can I say, no rest when a potential explosive device is involved."

"How about I don't charge you for this one, and you come back when you can," Henry offered. "And we can get a drink afterward."

"I'll text you to reschedule," Clara confirmed, but conveniently dodged the second part of his offer, as she hopped down from the massage table. She gestured towards the door with her head. "I need to change back into my clothes."

"What, you don't want an audience?"

She rolled her eyes. "Hardly; I'm way too private for that. Get out of here, Henry."

The masseuse did as she ordered, scurrying from the room. Once she was alone, she quickly changed back into her blue jeans and white t-shirt, pulled her hair into a bun, then grabbed her messenger bag before heading out of the spa.

Twenty minutes later, she arrived back at the Disaster City facility. She made her way over to the staging area outside the training center. Here, her fellow bomb detection handler, Ben Miller, was gathering up equipment and getting his dog into the kennel in the back of the DCSRA truck.

"Good, you made it back just in time," said Sergeant Young, the middle-aged head instructor of the facility. "Captain said we need to be ready to roll out in fifteen."

"I'll change quickly, grab Rebel, and be back in ten," Clara said, rushing past her superior.

She made a straight line for her apartment at the instructor villa where all of them lived. Clara stopped at the second set of townhomes, pulled out her keys, and unlocked the front door. She breezed inside and was greeted by the barking of her K9 partner, Rebel, from his kennel at the edge of the living room. "I'll come get you in just a few minutes, boy."

Clara rushed past the living room and kitchen combo area, heading down the small hall to where her bedroom and bathroom were located. She grabbed one of her blue cargo uniforms and slipped it on. Next, she pinned on her Disaster City Search and Rescue badge opposite her last name on the other side, and quickly shoved on and laced up her black combat boots.

As she re-entered the living room, Rebel was standing up in his kennel, his attention completely on Clara. "I know, boy, you're ready to go. Let me grab your leash." She picked it up from the nearby counter, opened the kennel door, and clipped it onto his collar. She patted him on the top of the head before guiding him towards the exit. "Come on, we have a new assignment. Let's put those expert skills of yours to work."

They made their way over to the staging area and loaded into the truck. The team arrived at the movie theater twenty minutes later, ready to walk the exterior of the property where the suspicious packages had been found. Clara and Rebel were assigned to the west side of the theater. Officer Miller, the other bomb detection instructor, took the east side with his K9 partner, Samson. Sarge stayed behind at the truck to coordinate from there.

Clara and Rebel made it about twenty yards before they came across the first package. From a distance, it looked like a shoe box wrapped in a bag. Clara removed Rebel's chew toy, then gave him the cue to inspect the box by sniffing it for the trace chemicals that would identify it as a bomb. When Rebel didn't sit down by it but returned to Clara's side instead, she knew it was safe to go over to the package and confirm her partner's dismissal of it as a threat. Sure enough, as she flipped the lid of the shoe box, there was just some old stuffing from shoes inside.

Clara wouldn't radio in her results yet, even though she was certain the area was clear of any other potential bombs. With this first one turning out to be nothing, she was beginning to think it might be a prank by kids. It wouldn't be the first time that a teenager would put a box by a public building then call in the threat to the place, thinking it would be funny. Often, they would sit across the street and watch the chaos of the target being evacuated.

They turned the corner at the edge of the building, and only walked another ten yards before another box came into view. This time, it looked to be a shipping box. Rebel did his job and quickly determined, with his keen sense of smell, it also was not a bomb. She looked inside to confirm it, but she knew Rebel wouldn't make a mistake. Up a little further, she saw a third box, followed by several more. As Rebel inspected each one, they quickly realized that all of them were empty. Then Clara noticed that behind a tree there was a shopping cart half-filled with cans and bottles, a sleeping bag, and a random assortment of more boxes filled with various objects. The collection of junk made it clear that the shopping cart had once belonged to a homeless person at some point. It looked abandoned now, almost as if whoever had been using it, had been chased off by someone else. In the chase, items had fallen out until it was abandoned completely. That would explain why there had been a trail of packages that led right to the cart.

Clara pressed the button on her radio. "All clear, there are no explosive devices. We found an abandoned shopping cart, most likely belonging to a homeless person. The boxes came from there."

"Roger that, Handler Burnette, come on back," Sergeant Young said over the radio. "Officer Miller didn't find anything on his end. We can let the movie theater know it's safe to resume business."

Clara bent down and rubbed between Rebel's ears. "Good boy, you earned this," she said, handing her partner a doggie treat. Once he gobbled it up, she gave him his favorite blue ball.

Immediately, Rebel's tail started wagging as he went to town on the chew toy.

By the time they returned to the academy, Clara was exhausted. At least she had one more day before the new trainees showed up. She was going to need it, too, because it was always hectic when a new class arrived.

# THREE

As Adam pulled through the gates of the Disaster City Search and Rescue facility, he was immediately taken aback by how big the place was. Multiple massive buildings were set on dozens of acres.

He climbed out of his truck, then went around to the passenger side and got Valor out. "You ready for this? I know it's scary, but we got this." Adam knew he was trying to convince himself as much as Valor. Though it was his dream to train at the elite academy, now that he was there, he hoped he didn't make a fool of himself.

"You must be one of the new trainees," a man with a thick New York accent, black hair, and gray eyes said, as he came up to Adam. "I'm Officer Joe

Griffin, one of the instructors here at DCSRA." The other man looked to be about a decade older than Adam and had an air of command around him like he'd seen a lot of action in his career.

"Nice to meet you, Officer Griffin. I'm Staff Sergeant Adam Reynolds, and this is my partner, Valor," Adam said, gesturing to the K9 next to him.

"We don't use rank or title around here on a regular basis, except when we call the Sergeant and Captain of our unit, Sarge and Cap. Other than that, we usually just use last names. It makes it a lot easier since we have instructors and trainees from all branches of the military including TSA and ATF, as well as police and sheriff departments across the country."

Adam nodded. "Understood."

"Man, you have military written all over you. It'll be good for you to get a little of that stiffness out of you," Joe said with a smirk.

"Let me guess, you're *not* military," Adam said, trying to hide his irritation at the man's obvious disapproval of his need to be respectful at all times due to his military training.

"No, I was a search and rescue officer in New York for twenty years before I got offered my position here at DCSRA."

"Twenty years?" Adam asked with surprise. "That means you were there for the search and rescue efforts for the Twin Towers, doesn't it?"

Joe's lighthearted nature that had been present previously disappeared at the mention of the towers. Instantly, Adam wished he had thought about it before he brought the subject up. "I'm sorry. I didn't mean to upset you."

"You would think after all these years, it would get easier to talk about, but it hasn't. That was, and will probably always be the hardest assignment of my career."

They were interrupted by the arrival of several more people driving up in their various vehicles joining the group in the parking lot. Joe told all of the new recruits to follow him. They made their way into the building that had a sign that read *Auditorium* across the top.

Adam took a seat in the second row towards the middle. As more and more recruits entered the building, he kept count. By the time the orientation meeting was moments from starting, fifty-two men and eight women had filled the rows around him. He couldn't tell much about any of them since they were in plain clothes like himself. He figured he would find out more about them and which departments they hailed from as his time in the academy progressed.

Twenty instructors filed onto the stage and made two rows. He noticed the team was almost all men with the exception of one petite brunette woman who stood at the end of the front row. Even though she was the only woman instructor, she didn't seem to let it affect her. She looked confident as she stood straight in her blue cargo uniform.

A gray-haired man with a face filled with wrinkles came forward. "Good morning, new trainees. I'm Captain Bill McCormick. I'm in charge of overseeing the elite Disaster City Search and Rescue Academy, better known as DCSRA. For all intents and purposes, our academy is an all-inclusive mini-city. This auditorium is used for orientation, guest lectures, and graduation ceremonies. We have a male and a female dormitory for trainees, as well as a set of apartment buildings and small houses for the permanent staff. We also have a cafeteria with a cook, a full gym with weight equipment and an indoor pool, and the Training Center that has several rooms for classes as well as the staff offices. Additionally, we have a fully staffed kennel and veterinarian hospital for our K9 partners, a permanent medical clinic, and a janitorial staff. What that means for each of you is that while you are here, you won't have any excuse to not meet and exceed the standards expected of you in order to graduate from our academy. Though this class is only one month long, I can assure you, it will be the most intense month of your life. It will test your limits, challenge what you think you know about search and rescue, and put you in situations you've never considered. I'm going to bring forward Master Sergeant Trevor Young, who will be overseeing the day-to-day operations of your class, to introduce the rest of the staff here at DCSRA."

The captain moved to the side, and a middle-aged man with salt-and-peppered brown hair came forward. "As the captain explained, I will be in charge of making sure each of you learn the latest techniques and skills by our highly-qualified instructors. When you finish your time here, you will be the top search and rescue officers and soldiers in the world. We have six areas of S & R with two instructors per division, plus an additional eight instructors assigned to specialized areas."

Adam quickly did the math and realized that meant for every three trainees, there would be one instructor. Every trainee would receive a lot of hands on guidance by the most elite teachers in their field.

"Officers Matthew Knight and Ray Carlson oversee narcotics training, Gunnery Sergeant Justin Ford and Officer John Lee run tracking and scouting, Officer Paul Smithen and Sergeant Major Juan Perez handle cadaver training, Officers Clara Burnette and Ben Miller are in charge of bomb detection."

Adam looked at the lone female instructor and realized that she would be one of the instructors directly overseeing his training. He wasn't sure what to think of that. Female K9 handlers were rare, let alone any that made it to the level that it took to become an instructor, especially at this elite academy.

"Officer Reggie Collins and Staff Sergeant Alex Murray provide training for missing persons, and Officers Sean West and Dylan Burke handle patrol and sentry training. The final eight instructors oversee specialized terrain training; Master Sergeant James Franklin and Officer Ross Canter train in the nearby mountains for avalanche and snow conditions while Mason Fredericks and Tom Powell train at the lake for water rescue. Finally, Officers Terrance Bilmont, Jesse Dixon, Rick Buckworth, and Joe Griffin oversee urban disasters such as terrorist attacks as well as natural disasters which include mudslides and earthquakes."

Sergeant Young spent the next half hour going over the rest of the staff at the facility, and the schedule for the first day. It was a long list of information. By the time it was over, Adam was glad it was time for them to head to the dorms and settle in for the night. He wasn't sure what the first day was going to bring when he woke up the next morning, but he knew that as long as he stayed true to himself and maintained his faith, he would be able to handle anything that came his way.

THE NEXT MORNING, ADAM AND VALOR LINED-UP with the other five men and their K9 partners. He wasn't sure what to expect from the bomb detection instructors, but he wanted to be ready for anything. He had pressed his DCSRA uniform and polished his boots the night before. Today, he wore it with pride, determined to finish the academy at the top of his class.

He glanced down the row of men. They all looked to be of various ages; the youngest man was probably in his late twenties and the oldest in his early forties. All of them wore their uniforms like him, but he noticed one of the men in the middle hadn't taken the time to iron his uniform. It wasn't his job to correct the other man, but he sure didn't think it made a good first impression.

As Adam waited for the instructors to arrive, he made sure to stand up straight, his chin lifted high. After all, he was representing the United States Army. He couldn't be anything less than professional.

"Good morning, trainees, welcome to your first day at the most elite, most prestigious bomb detection school in all the world," Instructor Miller said, coming to stand in front of the group. The female instructor, Burnette, joined him. "Let me make one thing clear, no matter how good you think you are at detection, no matter how many awards you've won or lives you've saved, none of that means anything here. Here, there is only one thing that matters. Our house, our rules. What that means is that everything you've learned and implemented over your career, you're going to set aside. We are the best of the best, which means we don't want to hear about how you do it at your department in Indiana, what you've learned from your time in

Afghanistan, or how you've read on the internet that a certain technique is the best. We have all the answers, we are the beginning and the end, the absolute authority on all things explosive—think of us as your all-knowing Mother and Father for the duration of your training."

Of all things to happen, Adam hadn't expected a *Top Gun* speech at their first meeting. What was this guy thinking? Was he trying to intimidate all of them? Was this a tactic to weed out anyone who wouldn't be able to handle the training? All of them had already been through a police academy or boot camp, plus bomb detection school by their various departments. There wasn't a need to make that type of speech; however, he knew better than to say anything. It wouldn't prove beneficial to infuriate his new instructor if he wanted to stay on his good side. Instead, he remained quiet, waiting to find out what was going to come next.

## FOUR

Clara sized up the six new trainees and their K9 partners standing in front of her. All of them seemed capable, but it was rare that a candidate was accepted into the academy who didn't present as such. When her eyes fell on one of the men in the middle who decided to show up for his first day in a wrinkled uniform, she realized she had a rare one standing in front of her who needed to be taught a lesson straight out of the gate.

She stepped forward to stand only inches in front of the man, narrowing her eyes. "Is there a reason you didn't feel the need to press your uniform?"

"Sorry, ma'am, I didn't realize we were going to

be judged on the condition of our uniform. I mean, we've already proven ourselves or we wouldn't be here."

"Instructor Burnette or Mother, if you prefer," she corrected. "And you should know, you're going to be judged on everything. If you can't take your appearance seriously, how can we expect you to take anything else we teach you seriously?"

The man shifted his stance, moving his weight from one leg to the other. He mumbled out, "It won't happen again."

"Good, because from the moment you step onto the DCSRA training grounds, you're going to be tested. It's only through our vigorous process that your true grit will be revealed. About a third of you will voluntarily quit, another third will barely squeak by, and the final third will flourish in this environment. It's up to you to determine which third you will end up being in."

Each of the men seemed to be taking in her words and contemplating them. She let the words sink in. They needed to know the odds they were facing in successfully completing this course.

Ben continued to go over training guidelines and what they would be expected to do every night to be prepared for the next day. As he went over their expectations, Clara continued to inspect the men. Besides Wrinkly—or Bernard as his name tag read across the left-side of his chest—there were two men older and younger than he was, along with a man who seemed to be the same age as she was. The older two men seemed cocky, which Clara knew Ben and she would easily be able to train right out of them; the younger ones looked scared. The one that piqued her interest though, was the final man. His name tag read, *Reynolds*. He seemed confident but not conceited. He was good-looking, too, but she quickly shook that thought from her head. As a woman in a mostly male-dominated profession, she knew it was never a good idea to get involved with a fellow bomb detector—even if the man in question might be the handsomest guy she'd ever laid eyes on.

"Today, we will start out in our mock airport terminal as a means to see what you and your K9 partners are capable of doing. We want to know what we are working with," Ben said with a stern look. "And like Mother said, you will be judged."

The group made their way into a room that was filled with a conveyor-belt that had suitcases, duffle bags, and car seats rolling around on it. There were also bicycles, shrink-wrapped pallets, golf bags, strollers, and wheelchairs scattered throughout the space.

"Here are the rules for this exercise. There are eight mock-bombs scattered throughout this area. You are to conduct your inspections and determine where they are without setting them off. There are decoys, and there are traps, so don't make a mistake or you'll regret it," Ben said as the instructors took their positions in the center of the room with their K9 partners.

The trainees were surrounding them, watching them, and Clara wondered if they were actually going to start. They did this the first time to see who had the initiative to get to work versus who sat back waiting to be told what to do.

Reynolds looked around the room. He kept glancing from the items to the instructors and back. Most of the other men kept their eyes on the instructors, but he was already sizing up what he should do. He must have decided to take a chance, because he quickly gave his K9 the command to search. They were off and working their way along the conveyor-belt of luggage pieces. His K9 partner was doing his job, checking for chemical vapors—or "volatiles"—that would give away a bomb to a K9.

Once Reynolds found the first bomb and

correctly identified it, the other five trainees scrambled to join him in the search. The team of dogs was searching the undersides and metal frames of each object in the room, moving along the rows.

She could hear the sniffing and snorting of the dogs as they eliminated objects and identified others that had mock-bombs inside them. The K9s' wagging tails coupled with their quick and eager searches made it clear this was their idea of a good time. If trained right, a bomb dog considered searching playtime rather than work. The key was to make sure they understood the rules of the game they were playing so no one got hurt accidentally.

The sudden popping sound drew her attention to one of the older trainees named Westerly. He was standing over a suitcase that had exploded and he was now covered in green paint. Apparently, he found one of the traps.

"Westerly, you're out," Ben said with a dissatisfied look on his face. "Go get cleaned up before mealtime."

The officer scurried off with his dog by his side, his head hanging low at the embarrassing demonstration of his capability. The rest of the teams continued searching. By the end of the exercise, most of the other teams fared better than Westerly, finding one bomb each except Foster. He didn't find any bombs but instead only decoys. At least he didn't set off a trap, which Clara supposed meant he did a little bit better than Westerly.

Two teams stood out with finding two bombs each, Reynolds and Rogers. They proved to be the most efficient of all the trainees. Clara was secretly impressed by both of them, but most of all Reynolds. He also didn't fall for any decoys while Foster's team was tricked by one. That one mistake could mean the difference between life and death, which meant Reynolds team had the rawest talent.

"Good job, trainees. Mother and Father approve of your work today," Ben said with a nod. "That concludes our first day of training. You're dismissed."

As Clara watched the teams file out, she wondered what the rest of the month was going to bring. Was this batch of recruits going to prove themselves worthy of being at DCSRA by learning important skills from them, or would they test them as they progressed through the training? Only time would tell.

## FIVE

The first week of training had come and gone, focusing on searching for traditional bomb components such as TNT, water gel and RDX, explosive powders, and dynamite. Adam was proving himself at the top of the heap every time they had a new exercise. It was a fine line to walk between shining bright and not causing his fellow bomb detectors to resent him. He didn't need to cause problems for himself by earning their animosity.

What he found most interesting was how he truly respected and admired both of his instructors. Miller could be smug and snarky sometimes, but he was also thorough and determined to show them how to be the best. Burnette was the perfect complement to Miller. She was a wealth of knowledge about everything to do with bombs and the various techniques to identify them. She was also methodical in implementing them. On top of it, she was easy on the eyes. He knew he shouldn't think of her that way, but he couldn't help himself. She was that gorgeous.

Over the past week, when no one was watching him, his gaze was drawn more and more to the beautiful brunette instructor. Her eyes twinkled when one of the teams did something right, which caused him to do as many things to perfection as he could. He loved putting that spark in them.

As Adam finished putting on his uniform, he refreshed his memory, going over the new techniques for searching for the chemical families of improvised explosives in his head. This week, they were switching focus which meant Valor would have to home in on urea nitrate, fertilizer, gunpowder, and hydrogen peroxide, the key components of IEDs. This was why Adam had wanted to come to DCSRA. He figured with the specialized, top-notch training under his belt, his superiors might be finally ready to send him overseas to work in the hot zones.

The dormitories were made up of individual rooms for each trainee so that they could keep their dog with them. Some trainees opted to let their dogs stay at the kennel, but Adam preferred keeping Valor with him. It was abnormal, considering the military frowned on handlers showing too much affection to their partners. There was a fear that a handler might choose to protect their dog or not put them in harm's way because of it. Adam thought just the opposite. He was certain it made them a better team.

Adam arrived at the classroom designated for the bomb detection group. He was the first to arrive and noticed that Instructor Burnette was busy lining up dozens of canisters at the back of the room. As she moved from one to the next, he couldn't help but notice how her uniform fit snuggly over her curvy body.

She glanced up and saw him staring at her. He could swear he felt his cheeks turn red with embarrassment. Quickly, he averted his eyes and hurried to one of the seats at the front with Valor sitting next to the chair.

"Is everything all right?" he heard her ask as she came up beside him. "You hurried off so quickly, it made me wonder if something was wrong."

Adam looked up at her, and his voice caught in his throat. She was looking down at him with those stunning brown eyes of hers, and he found himself at a loss for words.

"Is everything okay?" she asked with a confused look on her face.

He nodded, then cleared his throat. "Yes, I just didn't realize I was going to be early."

"I'd offer to let you help me with the canisters, but since you're already doing so well, I wouldn't want the other handlers to accuse you of having an unfair advantage by knowing what is in them."

He had a mixed reaction to her statement. Part of him was pleased that she noticed how well he was doing. He liked receiving her praise. The other part of him was disappointed he wouldn't have a chance to stand close to her as they arranged the canisters. It would have given him a chance to get to know her without anyone else around.

Adam tried to remind himself that none of those reactions was proper in his work environment. What was going on with him? He shouldn't be feeling this way about anyone, let alone his instructor. He should be focusing on his career. He was so close to getting his post overseas; he didn't need to blow it by getting caught up in an attraction to a woman who was clearly off-limits. He needed to focus on the nature of their relationship, not on the individual he was attracted to.

The rest of the teams and Instructor Miller showed up a few minutes later, filling in the seats around Adam. Part of him was relieved to no longer be alone with Burnette.

Instructor Miller took to the front of the room. "Good morning, trainees. I want to start off by telling you to be prepared for a physically and mentally exhausting day. All of you have had traditional IED training. Today, however, we are going to be training your dogs to learn to search for traditional IED elements combined with other abnormal components of explosive fuels such as confectioner sugar, bath salts, and baby powder. These variations are actually the challenging part of being able to identify and locate IED threats. Dogs need to learn when traditional chemicals are combined with rogue elements, it can still make a bomb."

Adam had read about this on the internet. He had wanted to stay current on the newest techniques for searching for IEDs; so much so, that he had been working on this very process during his time off. He had spent several weekends having Valor smell various combinations in their apartment, teaching him the differences.

Instructor Burnette came forward next giving more details. "It's important that your partners understand that despite the smell being mixed with something else, it can still go bang. We do this by exposing each dog to thousands of different explosive smells and thousands of different non-explosive ones. When your K9 partner deconstructs an odor into specific components, they're trained to pick out one culprit chemical. When there are other safe fuels that are mixed in, it can confuse the scent, making it one of the terrorist's best tactics. Let me give you a great analogy that will explain it. One of the experts in our field, likens it to salsa. When you walk into a kitchen and smell salsa being made, your nose says salsa. A dog's nose, on the other hand, doesn't recognize it as that. He instinctively registers it as tomatoes, onion, jalapeño, cilantro, and salt. You will be the ones to help your K9 partner understand its salsa, or in our world, a bomb."

"Any questions?" Instructor Miller asked, glancing at the five teams. Westerly already washed out, and decided to return to his post at his Air Force base. When everyone shook their heads, he continued. "Once we know your partners have a handle on the new smells, we will test your progress on the training ground."

They spent the next few hours having the dogs take turns smelling the various canisters. Some of the dogs picked up the scents better than others, but Valor far out-performed all of them due to his secret private training.

Once the classroom portion of the day was done, the group made their way to the rubble search grounds. Instructor Burnette and her K9 partner slowed down until she was walking next to Adam. "You did a great job in there, Reynolds. I was really impressed. We've never had a new trainee do that well. You have to tell me your secret."

Adam glanced around, making sure that no one else was listening to their conversation. "I read up about the new theories on IEDs and had been doing it on my own. I was hoping to have a chance to show my commanders and earn a position overseas."

"I read your file. Didn't you already serve overseas? Not many soldiers voluntarily want to go back for another deployment."

"Well, I feel like I owe it to my team. An IED took out my entire squad. Once I recovered from my injuries, I decided I wanted to cross-train into bomb detection to help keep it from happening to anyone else."

"That wasn't in your file," she pointed out.

"It was a classified mission at the time, so it never made it into my official file," he explained. "I worked reconnaissance, and while we were scouting an area, an IED planted in a bush went off."

"That's awful, Reynolds, I'm sorry that happened to your team. It speaks volumes about you that you decided to do this job in order to honor them."

They arrived at the urban rubble environment. It was the first time they would be working in the urban setting since arriving. He was looking forward to seeing how Valor responded when looking for IEDs.

The place was littered with broken down buildings, burnt out storefronts, and chunks of concrete. There were staircases that led to platforms and other buildings. There was an abandoned car and bus, as well as a playground.

"This is impressive," Adam marveled. "I can't believe the detail of this place."

"It helps to see how the dogs react in a replica of real-world environments while still maintaining safety," Instructor Burnette explained. "We get much more authentic results this way."

Within ten minutes of searching, Adam and Valor fell into a steady routine. He watched for his partner's cues that Valor had found something. After a few seconds, his K9 got really excited, and his tail wagged as his sniffing quickened and deepened. Adam knew that meant he had found something, causing him to be ready for his final alert. Sure enough, Valor sat down next to a piece of upturned concrete near the back corner of a staircase.

Adam moved forward to confirm Valor found an IED. When he saw the edge of something that didn't belong, he immediately raised his hand to signal they had a potential bomb.

Instructor Burnette came up nodding in approval. "Good job, Reynolds, you identified the first IED in the search area."

She moved on to check on the progress of a different team.

Bernard came up alongside Adam, a frown

making it clear he was irritated. "There you go again, showing off, and making the rest of us look like slackers. Man, could you be any more of a teacher's pet?"

"He can't help himself; he's hot for teacher," Colby added in a whisper as he came up behind them. "Haven't you seen the way he looks at her when he thinks no one is watching? He totally has it bad."

"Is that right, Reynolds? Are you into Instructor Burnette?" Bernard questioned.

Adam shook his head adamantly, not liking the two of them ganging up on him. "No, I just like doing my job to the best of my abilities, which is what the two of you should be worried about, not my lack-of-love life. Get back to searching before you get us all into trouble."

Colby rolled his eyes. "Nice deflection, Reynolds, but don't think this isn't getting brought up later. We're definitely getting to the bottom of it."

Adam didn't like the sound of that. The last thing he wanted was for the other guys to be pestering and harassing him about his apparently obvious attraction to their instructor.

"What's going on here? There shouldn't be any

talking; it could set off a device," Instructor Burnette snapped at the group. "I have a good mind to kick the three of you out of here simply on principle."

"We'll stop right now," Adam said, giving a withering glare to the other two men for getting him into trouble.

"Good, because if you ever act like this in a live scenario, you might not get a second chance. Get back to searching."

At the end of the day, as Adam was packing up his bag, he overheard Bernard complaining to Instructor Miller.

"I just don't get it. She sees fire everywhere when there isn't even smoke. Why is she like that?"

"It's what makes Mother a great bomb detector, not to mention teacher," Instructor Miller explained. "She's usually three steps ahead of everyone else. And for the record, if you ever try to come between Mother and Father again, you'll disappear from this academy faster than a toupee in a hurricane."

Adam quietly left the training area, not wanting them to know he overheard their conversation. Why was Bernard so mad at Instructor Burnette? She hadn't done anything Instructor Miller wouldn't have done. Was it because she was a woman? Was it because of what he perceived was going on between Adam and her? If that was the case, he needed to figure out a way to let go of his attraction to her before it got them both into a whole mess of trouble. The problem was, he didn't know how

**B**en had warned the trainees they would be tired when the day was over, but what he left out was that it took a toll on the instructors, too. Clara felt like every muscle was hurting at the moment. What she wouldn't give for a massage from Henry, but she knew that was out of the question.

She reached up and rubbed the back of her neck, trying to ease the knot away that had formed between her shoulder blades.

"I could use one of those, too," she heard Reynolds' familiar voice say from behind her. He came up beside her, holding his tray of food. She glanced up from the cafeteria table, and immediately regretted making eye contact with him. He looked great in his DCSRA uniform, but he looked even better in his civilian clothes. He had on a pair of blue jeans and a black t-shirt. His muscles were poking out from the edges of the sleeves and she could swear she saw the edge of a tattoo. She didn't know why, but she was curious to know what he had inked on his upper arm. Not just because it would tell her more about him, but because it would mean she would get to see him without a shirt on. The idea of that was more appealing than she cared to admit, even to herself.

"Maybe I should make a suggestion for us to hire a masseuse for the academy," she teased. "I wonder how that would go over."

"Probably not that great," he said, sitting down at the table across from her. It was the first time any of the trainees had crossed the boundary when they were off-the-clock. Not that it couldn't happen, but they usually stuck together and left the instructors to themselves.

"You sure you want to add fuel to the fire?" Clara asked, glancing around the room. "I mean, they already think you're the teacher's pet."

"You heard about that?"

She shrugged. "It's why I broke that huddle up earlier today. I mean, it really could have set off a device, but I did it more to get you away from them."

"Thanks for that," he said with a grin. "I was really uncomfortable. You didn't have to be so harsh with me though, when it wasn't even my fault."

"Hey, I wasn't about to make it worse for you. I had to make it look like I was treating you all the same."

"I don't think it's going to help. They want to believe I don't deserve my top spot in the rankings."

"Don't worry about it. They're just suffering from professional jealousy. You're out-performing all of them, and they hate it. They'll do anything to get under your skin."

"Well, it's working," he admitted, looking over to meet her eyes. "I don't want anyone to think that I'm getting praise and accolades if I don't deserve them."

"That's just it, you do. Don't doubt yourself, Reynolds. You're one of the most naturally gifted handlers I've seen in years. You were built for this job."

A few more people joined their table. The meal passed with everyone talking about their day. By the time they were all finished, the trainees were ready to go relax in the recreational center.

"You coming?" Reynolds asked, lagging behind the group to invite her.

She shook her head. "No, it's frowned upon for instructors to fraternize with trainees." It wasn't a complete lie. Her fellow instructors would definitely comment if she did, especially if she was hanging out with the trainee who was at the center of rumors circulating about her favoritism.

Clara wished she could deny the rumors outright, but the problem was, part of her did favor Adam. Not just because he was the best trainee at the academy—because he was—but also because she found him insanely attractive. It was best if she didn't engage with him outside training anymore. It would be the only way for her to keep it as professional as possible.

"I need to head back to my apartment. I'll see you tomorrow, Reynolds."

The look of disappointment was clear on his face, and for a moment, she almost changed her mind. Then she found a new well of resolve and turned to walk away. If she didn't watch out, he was going to become a real problem for her.

## SEVEN

The second week was ending. Another trainee had washed out after having a difficult time with IEDs, leaving just four to finish out the rest of the month. To celebrate surviving half the training, their instructors decided that a good old-fashioned competition was in order. They were split into teams designated by Sarge and both led by one of their instructors.

To Adam's surprise, he was assigned to Instructor Burnette's team. He hadn't expected it, but he could say he was glad about it. He liked the idea of working closely with her while showing off his skills to her again.

"Here are the rules," Instructor Miller said to the group that was standing in the middle of the crashed airplane training grounds. "Teams will search for bombs which will be a mix of traditional explosive devices and IEDs. Before anyone complains, we didn't hide the bombs. Sarge did that so it would be fair. He will also be monitoring the competition to make sure there isn't any cheating. This will be timed, but don't make mistakes because of it. Like always, there will be traps and decoys. If you set off a trap, you're out. If you get tricked by a decoy, you're also out. My suggestion, take your cues from Mother and Father since we always know best."

Sarge raised his arm, then dropped it as he clicked the stopwatch on in his other hand. The teams took off in opposite directions. At first, both teams followed their instructors, but as more and more bombs were found, the remaining men became cocky.

Bernard was the first one to have a trap explode in his face. Adam had to admit, even though it left his team at a disadvantage, it was worth it just to see him covered in blue paint. He did find two actual bombs before that happened, but as Instructor Miller explained, he was out. That meant it was up to Adam and Instructor Burnette to keep their lead. Easier said than done with the other team breathing down their necks with an extra man. Within a few minutes, they had nearly caught up to Adam's team with only one bomb to tie, and two to win.

Adam was beginning to worry. Despite the fact they had found five bombs, with a one man disadvantage, it wasn't going to be enough. The classic sound of popping made Adam's heart sing. He glanced across the training ground and noticed that Colby was covered in blue paint, just like Bernard. The teams were even again. Adam's team could take this if, they found just one more bomb; however, Adam knew better than to rush. If he did that, he could fall for a trap or decoy, and then that would leave Instructor Burnette by herself. He didn't want to do that to her. Not that she wasn't capable on her own, but he wanted to help her win.

Out of the corner of his eye, Adam watched as Rogers fell for a decoy and had to leave the competition. That meant that Adam was the only trainee left. He'd already found two bombs, tying him for the second most found by a trainee. Adam really wanted to find one more so he could have the most. He noticed that the edge of a passenger seat from the airplane seemed "off" to him. He guided Valor over and let him inspect the area. To Adam's great pleasure, his suspicion had been right. Valor sat down next to a box that had been hidden under the seat. Adam raised his hand to signal they found a bomb.

"And that's time," Sarge declared. "With that bomb, Burnette's team won with seven devices safely located."

"Congratulations," she said, patting Adam's arm. Her touch shocked him, causing him to feel off kilter. He hadn't expected the physical contact from her, and though he liked it, he didn't know what to make of the warmth it caused to ripple up his arm.

Adam stumbled back, tripping over the edge of one of the nearby passenger chairs. He couldn't rectify himself in time, and he went crashing into some rubble. His foot remained behind, stuck between the chair and a piece of metal. He let out a loud yelp of pain.

"Someone go get the doctor," Instructor Burnette barked out with worry written across her face. "Don't move, Reynolds. You might make it worse."

He wanted to try to get free, but he knew she was right. If he had any chance of not making it worse, he needed to lay still.

"It's going to be okay," she whispered, reaching

out and placing her hand on his chest in an effort to calm him. Little did she know, it actually caused his heart to speed up. "Dr. Stine is excellent. He'll know what to do."

After the doctor arrived and inspected his injuries, Adam found out he only suffered from a few bumps and bruises for the most part. His worst injury was a bruised ankle. It didn't mean he had to go home, but he definitely needed to rest it over the weekend.

"You're lucky. It could have been a lot worse," Instructor Burnette said with a sigh. "For being so good at bomb detection, I don't see how you managed to trip over something as trivial as a piece of metal."

"I think he was distracted," Colby pointed out, wagging his eyebrows up and down in a way that made it clear he thought he knew something about what had caused Adam to trip.

"Look, I'm pretty exhausted. I just want to get back to my room and lay down," Adam said, ignoring Colby's annoying behavior.

The group made their way out of the training grounds and headed towards the main campus. Before they reached the dormitory though, the Captain was there with a piece of paper in his hands. "Your team has a hot call. It turns out, there is a bomb threat at an outdoor mall with multiple packages spotted around the area."

"I hate to say this, Reynolds, but you're going to have to stay behind with your ankle like that," Sarge said with a shake of his head. "I'm sorry about this. I'm sure you would like to go with your team, plus you would have been a real asset."

Adam's heart sank at the news. Of all the days to twist his ankle, it had to be on the one day they got an active call.

"He shouldn't stay on his own. The trainees need the experience and only one instructor needs to go with them. I'll stay with Reynolds and you can go with them, Miller."

A momentary look of disapproval crossed Instructor Miller's face before he quickly covered it up. He nodded, saying, "Team, go change into clean uniforms and grab whatever you need for you and your partner. Meet me back here in ten minutes. We'll load up in the bomb truck and take off in twenty."

Adam wasn't sure what to make of Instructor Burnette's offer to stay with him. If he didn't know any better, he would have sworn her decision didn't go over well with her colleague. Did Miller suspect something was going on between Adam and her? There wasn't. Well, not officially, that was. Adam got the distinct impression that if they were in any other situation, he would have kissed her already, and she would have let him. With her staying to take care of him, was there a chance that maybe that could happen anyway?

## EIGHT

While the rest of the team was off checking out the shopping mall threat, Clara was sitting next to Adam in his dormitory apartment. He was resting on his bed with Valor beside him. Clara had kenneled Rebel, wanting to make sure she was free to focus on helping Adam with whatever he might need.

"How are you feeling? Do you need any more pain meds?"

Adam shook his head. "I'm fine," he muttered out as he shifted his position. He pushed back against the stack of pillows behind him. It didn't seem to do the trick. He turned around and picked up the closest one, smashing it between his hands a couple of times before slinging it back down, slumping back against them with a pout on his face.

"You don't look fine," Clara pointed out. "What's wrong?"

He drew in a deep breath and held it before speaking. "I just hate being hindered. I want to be out there with everyone else doing my job," he admitted, the frustration clear in his voice. "How else am I going to be able to put these new skills I've learned to the test?"

"I get that, but you'll have plenty of time to do that down the road."

"Not here, not where I can make a name for myself that will hopefully carry back to my superiors. I'm not getting any younger, and if I want to get an assignment over in a hot zone, I need that."

"Just so you know, I plan on writing a glowing letter of recommendation for you. I can't promise anything with it; however, they usually carry a lot of clout since I've been an instructor here for over five years. I know what I'm talking about."

"Thank you," Adam said with a smile. "I really appreciate that. I didn't mean to guilt you into anything though."

She shook her head. "You didn't. I had already made up my mind to do it a few days ago. Like I've told you before, you're one of the best handlers I've had the privilege of working with. I know I'm supposed to be training you, but truthfully, I've even picked up a few tricks by watching you."

"You've been watching me?"

Clara shifted in her chair beside his bed. She didn't want to admit it to herself, let alone him, but it was more than that. There was an attraction to him that she couldn't explain. Not only was he devastatingly handsome, but she really liked him the more she got to know him. Deciding to give herself an out, she said, "It's my job."

"Oh, is that all?" a look of disappointment settled on his face. "Is there any way we can start calling each other by our first names? It's seems ridiculous to call you Instructor Burnette now that we've become friends."

"Is that what we are now?" she asked, arching one of her eyebrows. "I didn't get the memo."

"I thought we were. I figured that was why you decided to stay here with me rather than going on the call, Clara."

She liked the way her name rolled off his tongue. It was like it was as easy as picking out a favorite outfit to wear, warm and intimate. She immediately decided she liked it. "You can call me by my first name when we're in private."

"Then you should call me Adam."

"To clarify why I stayed, Adam, I've gone on plenty of calls over the years. There'll always be more bomb threats despite our best efforts to stop them. Besides, someone needed to keep an eye on you."

"One of the other trainees or instructors could have done that. Was there another reason you decided to stay?"

Clara wasn't sure how to answer him. She knew there was more to it than what she had been admitting, but she wasn't about to tell him that. Trying to avoid giving an answer to the probing question, she changed the subject by standing up and saying, "You're starting to sweat a bit, which means the pain is higher than you're letting on. Why don't I go grab you a couple of pills and a glass of water?"

When she returned with his meds, she had decided to surprise Adam with a special trip. "I have somewhere I want to take you. It's going to do you a world of good."

"Where's that?"

"Let's just say it's better if I just show you."

Adam shrugged. "If it means I get to spend more time with you, I'm in."

Clara felt her cheeks blush at the flirtatious compliment. She liked that he wanted to spend time with her, and despite the warnings she kept giving herself, she liked being with him, too.

Clara took Valor over to the kennel and checked him in for the afternoon. She came back to collect Adam, who had switched out of his sweats and into a pair of jeans. Once he was settled inside her car, she went around to the driver's side, excited to show him her favorite place to go. Twenty minutes later, they were pulling up in front of The West Side Spa and Salon.

"You brought me to a hair salon? Are you trying to tell me you don't like my hair cut?" Adam asked with confusion, as he lifted his hand to his military high-and-tight.

"No, your hair is fine. We're here for the other part."

"The spa?" he asked with incredulousness. "Why on earth would I need to go in there?"

"Because, considering what you just went through, a massage is exactly what you need."

"Couldn't you just give me one?"

"I could, but I'm not nearly as good as Henry.

Besides, I already texted him and told him we were on our way. He arranged for us to have side-by-side massages."

"Who's Henry?" Adam asked in a way that made it clear he was jealous of the other man.

"My masseuse—just my masseuse, though he's made it clear he would be interested in more."

"Can't say I blame him. Any man would be a fool to not want more with you. I have to admit though, I'm glad to hear it's one-sided. I would hate to find out you have a boyfriend."

"Nope, no boyfriend. The only guys that take up time in my life are Father and Rebel."

She wanted to add Adam to the list, but she was afraid it would reveal too much about how she felt about him. It was better to keep that information to herself. She knew it couldn't go anywhere, so she didn't want to encourage him to pursue her in any way.

They entered the spa and the hostess greeted them with a friendly smile, offering them both a glass of cucumber water. Her eyes lingered on Adam a little longer than Clara would have preferred, but it wasn't surprising since he was so handsome. Who wouldn't want to stare at him?

They made their way to the back where Henry

was waiting with another female masseuse. "Good to see you, Clara. This is Jessica and she'll be working on your...*friend*."

The way Henry said the last word made it clear he wasn't sure what their relationship was.

"He's one of my recruits," Clara quickly clarified. "He was beat up pretty badly during our last exercise, so I thought it would do him good to bring him here for a massage."

"I'll take good care of him," Jessica said, giving Adam a little-too-eager smile.

Clara didn't like that. She didn't want some woman making the massage more personal than it needed to be. Deciding to put a stop to that, she said, "I was actually thinking you should work on him, Henry. You do such a great job on me; I want him to have the best. No offense, Jessica."

It was clear the other woman was perturbed. The smile disappeared as she flippantly said, "Whatever you want; you're the client."

"Why don't you both follow us this way," Henry suggested, interjecting himself before the conversation could get out of hand. He must have noticed the tension between Clara and the other woman.

They made their way to a large room that had two massage tables ready for them.

"We'll leave the two of you to change," Jessica said, gesturing with her head to Henry that they should leave. Henry didn't seem to like it, but he did it anyway.

They both moved behind the changing areas and slipped on the robes provided. When Adam re-emerged, she could see that the tattoo that she had been wondering about must move up his shoulder and finished at the edge of his chest.

"I have to ask, what do you have tattooed?"

Adam glanced down, then slowly pulled back the edge of his robe to reveal his arm and chest. Clara's heart clenched at the sight of his golden, chiseled chest. She moved closer to inspect the tattoo.

"Death before Dishonor," she read above the insignia of the Army. There were also several letters spread throughout the design.

"What do the letters stand for?" she said, her hand reaching out to trace them.

"Those are the initials of the soldiers I lost during my last deployment."

"It's stunning," she whispered, letting her fingers linger on his muscles.

There was a knock from the other side of the

door, causing them to pull apart just as Henry and Jessica came back into the room.

"Are we doing the standard massage today, Clara?" Henry asked.

"Let's go with the works. Adam's earned it."

The two masseuses spent the next hour using therapeutic lotions and hot rocks on their bodies, as well as rubbing out every tight muscle.

"You were right," Adam conceded, "this is amazing."

"After a long month of training new recruits, this is my treat to myself. Of course, I don't tell the other instructors about this. They would never understand and only make fun of me for it."

"Why did you decide to trust me enough to bring me here then?"

"I don't know. It's just a gut instinct that you're different. I just had a feeling you wouldn't be like the other guys I work with."

"Thanks for trusting me enough to share this," Adam said. "Your secret is safe with me."

Once they were finished with the massage, Clara changed back into her clothes and excused herself to go to the restroom. Outside in the hall, Henry stopped her. "What are you doing with that guy, Clara?"

"What are you talking about? I told you, he's one of my trainees."

"I'm not arguing that, but it's clear, he's not *just* your trainee. Tell me you didn't make the mistake of getting involved with him."

"I'm not sure what you're getting at, but nothing is going on. Honestly, Henry, jealousy is an ugly color on you."

"I'm not going to deny that it makes me jealous to watch you with him. I can see the looks you give him when you think no one is watching. That's not the reason I'm objecting though. I'm worried what this would do to your career if it got out. You tell me all the time how they already treat you differently because you're a woman. How do you think it would go over if they found out you were involved with him?"

Clara had been worried about the same thing. It was why she kept telling herself not to develop feelings. The problem was, she was already past that point. Her attraction to Adam had turned into something more, and she didn't know what to do about it.

"I have to go, Henry. We have to get back before the rest of the team returns from a call."

After finishing up in the restroom, Clara

returned to the massage room. Adam was back in his civilian clothes, and for a moment, she was disappointed. She liked seeing him in the robe because it exposed his chiseled chest. Now, it was covered up by a white t-shirt, which was probably for the best since she shouldn't be thinking about him that way. She might not like why Henry objected to her feelings for Adam, but he was right; Adam was strictly off-limits.

"We need to head back." She turned around, but before she could get away, she felt Adam's hand reach out and grab her arm. He pulled her back towards him and before she knew what was happening, his mouth met hers. The kiss was explosive, like the strongest bomb she could ever imagine going off right between them. It pulsated with intensity, causing her to shake with shocked elation. She could feel her heart beating faster, the need to be close to him overriding every sensible part of her. She let her hands move up and wrap around his neck as he deepened the kiss.

Suddenly, there was a knock at the door, interrupting the moment. Remembering who she was kissing, she quickly pulled back in shame. "I shouldn't have let that happen. It was a mistake." This time when she turned around to leave, she made sure to keep going. Though she knew for certain now she had feelings for Adam, she also knew she was going to have to avoid him as much as possible once they got back to the academy. No one would ever understand how she fell for one of her trainees, so she had to do whatever it took to keep anyone from finding out, especially Adam.

# NINE

Adam couldn't stop thinking about the kiss he'd shared with Clara. It had been impulsive, and completely driven by the need to show her how much he cared. The problem was, the moment she pulled away, he saw the embarrassment in her eyes, and Adam regretted it. The last thing he had wanted to do was upset her.

Now she was avoiding him. They were firmly into the middle of the third week, and every time he tried to strike up a conversation with her, she would treat him like he was any other trainee. Though he knew there was nothing he could do about it, her reaction to him since their kiss still hurt.

Today, they were working on searching unusual

items for explosives. This would work well in his wheelhouse of skills and look great on his resume for when he applied to be stationed overseas in a hot zone. He'd be able to show that he was capable of finding hidden and complex IEDs.

"Remember, trainees, you want to make sure to guide your K9 partner to inspect the most hidden places. Don't forget the lining of purses, suitcases, golf bags. You also want to look under large objects where the heavier-than-air vapors settle," Clara reminded them.

"You've only got a few minutes left. Make them count. The more bombs you find, the more lives you save," Instructor Miller added.

Though the words of his instructor sounded urgent, Adam willed himself not to rush. Rushing was a handler's worst instinct. It could cause them to make a mistake that would harm both him and his partner, not to mention anyone unfortunate enough to be close to the blast radius.

There was a wrapped pallet that caught Adam's eye. He directed Valor over to the area, then let his K9 go to work. Single sniffs and snorts became double, then triple, and it quickly became clear Valor had found something. As his tail started to wag back and forth, Adam knew before he sat down that there was a bomb under the pallet. He raised his hand to signal to the instructors that they had found an explosive device.

"Great work, Reynolds. Father is exceptionally proud of you. That's your sixth bomb for this exercise," Instructor Miller praised as he came up next to Adam. "And by my calculation, the best any handler has ever done here. You've set a trainee record at DCSRA. There's still a few minutes in this round, which means you might be able to make it seven."

Instructor Miller moved on, leaving him to start searching again. Adam glanced over at Clara, who was busy validating one of Colby's finds. Even though she had been closer to Adam, she had avoided coming over, which bothered Adam to no end. It was one thing to avoid him personally, but professionally was a whole other thing. He'd just broken a record, and she didn't even care enough to congratulate him.

"Good job, Reynolds," Bernard said. "I guess all that private time with Instructor Burnette over the weekend really paid off."

"Why don't you focus on searching rather than on me," Adam suggested, giving the other man a dark look of anger. "I don't care for your asinine comments all the time."

"Don't take it personally. I mean, any one of us would hit that if given the opportunity," Colby added, before turning around with his K9 partner and taking off.

It took all of Adam's energy to keep from marching over to Colby and punching him square in the jaw. He didn't like the other man talking about Clara that way or implying that he was using her like that. He knew he couldn't hit him though, so instead he distracted himself by searching again.

A few minutes later, there was the recognizable popping sound of one of the traps going off. Adam turned around to see who got sprayed with paint. It was Rogers, but something was wrong. He was screaming out in pain and had fallen to the ground. The rest of the teams and Clara rushed over to his side. Instructor Miller was bent down beside him, asking, "Can you see, Rogers?"

"It hurts, it hurts!" he cried out, as he writhed in pain on the floor. He had his hands over his eyes and Adam quickly realized he wasn't wearing his protective goggles.

"Did the trap explode in your eyes?" Clara

asked with concern, but Rogers couldn't answer. He only continued to cry out in pain.

"I was nearby and watched it happen," Bernard said. "Rogers bent down to see behind the corner of the staircase and his goggles came loose. Then the trap went off."

Clara shouted over her shoulder, "Colby, go get the doctor right now. Tell him there was an accident and that it's an emergency."

Colby rushed off in the direction of the medical clinic. Rogers wasn't calming down, but instead was crying out in more pain. The way the other man was reacting, took Adam right back to the time when the IED detonated in the middle of his squad. He remembered the men, who hadn't been killed by the initial explosion, were writhing around on the ground, screaming out in pain. Rogers was behaving just like that.

Adam's palms started to sweat, he could feel his heart speed up so fast he thought he might pass out, and the room was starting to tilt. Valor whined, and moved closer to Adam's side, nuzzling against his partner's leg. He must have sensed what was going on with Adam.

"I'll go check on Colby," Adam said, turning around to take off without waiting to be dismissed.

He couldn't stay there a moment longer, or he was going to melt down right in front of everyone. He couldn't let that happen.

Adam only got about halfway to the clinic when he saw Colby and Dr. Stine coming towards him. "Has he gotten worse?" Colby asked with worry.

"He's about the same," Adam stated, then looking at the doctor, he added, "It looks bad, Doc, really bad. I'm worried he might lose his eyesight."

"We'll do all we can, but you all know the risks when you sign up for this job," Dr. Stine said. "There's always a chance, even in training, something will go wrong."

Adam made his way back to the dormitory, heading straight to his room. He needed to lay down to wait until this panic attack passed. They didn't happen often, but when they did, he could be laid up for days. He couldn't afford for that to be the case while he was at DCSRA. They'd kick him out for sure. He needed to figure out a way to get this under control before it was too late.

As he lay in his bed with Valor next to him, he patted his partner's head, trying to let their bond soothe him. Adam went over the techniques the Army psychologist suggested to help calm his nerves, but they weren't working as well as he would've hoped. Knowing he needed more help, he sent up a silent prayer asking God to intervene. Finally, a peace started to take hold in his heart. The symptoms started to subside, and Adam could feel the tension leaving his body. Thank goodness. The last thing he wanted to have happen was to leave DCSRA under such horrible circumstances. That would most definitely keep him from getting an assignment in a hot zone.

Rather than think about his squad or Rogers, Adam forced himself to think about something positive. The first thing that popped into his head was Clara's face. She was the final key to calm him. As he drifted off to sleep, her beautiful face was his last conscious thought.

# TEN

After Rogers was loaded onto a gurney and was taken to the clinic, Clara headed back towards the instructors' villa. She needed to take a shower and then get some sleep. Not only was it difficult watching Rogers suffer like that, but she was worried about Adam. She could justify her concern as his instructor, but it went beyond that. She cared what was going on with him as she recognized she had strong feelings for him. It was why she had pulled away after their kiss. Letting herself get romantically involved would be a big mistake—one she couldn't afford. She needed to keep their relationship strictly professional. Even as she tried to convince herself of that fact, however, rather than returning to her own apartment, she found herself heading towards the male dormitory. Knowing Adam's back story concerning his squad in Afghanistan, she was certain he was suffering from a panic attack due to PTSD. There was nothing about it in his file, but it wouldn't be the first time mental medical history was kept out of a dossier about a soldier so it wouldn't affect their career. If that were the case, it would be in both their best interests if she checked on him, wouldn't it? After all, she was his instructor, which meant she was responsible for his well-being. Happy with her own justification for her course of action, she hurried up her cadence as she silently sent up a prayer that everything would go well with Adam when they talked.

Clara arrived at Adam's room and softly knocked on the door.

"Who is it?" she heard him shout from the other side.

"It's Clara. May I come in?"

"Sure."

She opened the door and went inside. She moved through the living area to the bedroom where he was sitting up in bed. He looked pale and disoriented, like he wasn't even sure where he was and why.

"Are you okay?" she asked, pulling a chair over to sit down next to him.

"I'm fine," he said, giving the same answer he always did. "You should be worried about Rogers, not me."

"He's been flown via helicopter to the best hospital in Dallas. They'll be able to help him. What I'm worried about now is you, Adam. What happened to you today?"

"It doesn't matter. I've got it under control now."

"Look, I know you might be worried that I will put this in a report or tell somebody, but that's not the case. I'm here as your friend, not as your instructor. I want to make sure you're all right."

"I am now, but I wasn't earlier. Ever since my squad was killed in the roadside bombing, I've battled with PTSD. I've had to fight against depression, anxiety, and panic attacks. Even though it's not officially in my record, I think that's why they haven't given me a position in a hot zone. They're worried I won't be able to handle the stress of it."

"I think you need to cut yourself some slack,"

Clara coaxed, reaching out and placing her hand on top of his. "You did pretty well today, considering all that happened. You kept your composure, and when you found a chance to leave, you did it without drawing attention. I know a lot of trainees without PTSD, that would have done far worse than that."

"Thank you, Clara," he whispered, her name causing her stomach to flip-flop at the sound of it. "I needed to hear that. I want so badly to serve in a way that honors the fellow soldiers I lost, but I worry that's never going to happen. I feel like my PTSD keeps getting in the way."

"You shouldn't be ashamed of it, Adam. You have it because you survived something that most soldiers never have to go through. You're brave, strong, and resilient. You're exactly what the military needs for a soldier fighting on the front line."

The words were true, and she believed them, but it didn't keep her from hating the idea of him being across the world from her. She was beginning to see that she didn't like the idea of Adam leaving DCSRA. She had gotten used to him being there and didn't look forward to a time when he wouldn't be.

"I'll try not to let it get me down," Adam promised. "I really appreciate you coming to check on me."

"You're welcome. Glad to do it."

"I have one other matter I wish to discuss with you," Adam said, looking her straight in the eyes. "This whole 'friend' thing; it's not working for me."

Clara's heart sank. With the end of his training approaching, it seemed Adam was ready to move on. He had been clear he was doing all of this to get an assignment overseas. She wasn't sure why it bothered her so much.

"I'm sorry to hear that. I really thought there was something between us. I must have been mistaken."

"Wait, that's not what I meant. What I meant was that I don't want to be *just* friends. I like you Clara, and if you're interested, I'd like to explore whether or not this could be something more." He leaned forward and placed his hand on the side of her cheek. "I *want* this to be something more." His lips claimed hers for his own. This kiss was different than the first, filled with a desire and passion that made Clara's body quiver with excitement. She'd almost objected to his declaration, but at the moment, she was ready to relent and let their relationship evolve into something more. She wasn't sure how things were going to work out between them, but she was certain of one thing—kissing Adam Reynolds had firmly taken the position as her favorite thing to do.

## ELEVEN

The third week finished with just Bernard, Colby, and Adam remaining. Though Rogers was going to heal and not lose his eyesight, the recovery was going to take months. He wasn't going to be able to return to the academy to finish with them. The captain did, however, offer him a slot in any future class once he was cleared for full-duty again.

As they started their fourth and final week, Adam felt pleased with the fact that he was continuing to hold his position as the top performer of not only the bomb detection class, but of the entire academy. He'd met all the benchmarks set forth by the academy and had broken multiple records. On top of his training going well, he was forming something with Clara. They hadn't defined what it was yet, but he was hoping it would lead to something permanent once they could go public with their relationship.

"Trainees, as we approach the end of your time here at DCSRA, we've decided to save the best for last," Instructor Miller said with pride. "You will be working in tandem with the other search and rescue training teams in a mock massive terrorist disaster. You will have live victims trapped in the rubble, fake bombs which can go off and do real damage if not handled properly, and simulated hurricane weather conditions to contend with. All of it on your own without Mother and Father to guide you. This *will* test your mettle in a way no other scenario ever has. This will be your final chance to prove yourself ready to be called a DCSRA graduate."

Adam wanted nothing more than to work well with the other teams and bring in the top honors from the final exercise. If he could do that in such a stressful environment, he could prove he was capable of handling a hot zone assignment.

"Today, we are going to go over what will be expected and how to work in a multi-faceted search and rescue effort. It will be chaotic; you will feel pressure to speed up your process, but you will need to remember your training—" Clara didn't finish her sentence as her eyes darted to the back of the classroom. "Excuse us for a moment. Sarge needs to speak with us."

Clara and Instructor Miller disappeared towards the back. They were taking turns talking. When Sarge was talking, they would listen and nod, then respond with a few gestures towards the trainees. Whatever was going on, it involved Adam and his fellow trainees. Had something else happened?

Their instructors came back to the front of the classroom. Instructor Miller explained what was going on. "There has been a pipe bomb that was detonated in a mailbox in the nearby town of Woody. Luckily, no one was injured, but there is concern that more have been planted around the area. The bomber sent a note, claiming this was only the first one. We've been called out to search for any devices. We'll be coordinating with the Dallas detection teams and bomb squad, who will detonate any devices we find."

"You have fifteen minutes to grab anything you might need, after which you are to report to the staging area outside the training center," Clara added.

The trainees took off with their K9 partners, making their way straight to the dormitory to gather their equipment. Once Adam had everything he needed loaded up in his work bag, he headed over to the meet-up location. The place was in a flurry with both of his instructors, as well as his fellow trainees, putting their bags and dogs into the kennel in the back of their DCSRA truck.

Thirty minutes later, the team arrived in Woody. The staging area for the task force was filled with uniformed officers, and newspaper reporters that were roped off several yards away. The Dallas bomb squad had already arrived.

The bomb squad captain was going over a map laid out on the hood of one of the police cars. "Good, the DCSRA team is here. We've assigned each of your teams to work in tandem with three officers in each grid area. If you find anything, send someone back to bring in the bomb detonation team. Do not approach or make contact with the potential device, and remember, stay off your radios. The signal could set off a nearby bomb."

Adam could feel the anticipation building inside him. He'd only checked cars for bombs at the base. He'd never had a chance to search for bombs in a real-world situation. If he could handle this, it would prove his PTSD wouldn't be a problem. This was a make or break moment for him.

Adam and Valor were assigned with one Woody and one Dallas officer. They were working the area together, making sure to spread out far enough to cover more ground, but not too far as to miss anything. Any time one of the cops found something suspicious, they would signal for Adam and Valor to investigate.

Their training kicked in, and Adam and Valor moved together in unison. They knew exactly what to look for, unlike his counterparts that thought innocuous objects such as trash cans and bird feeders might be bombs. Valor cleared object after object the other two cops continued to point out. As he deemed each one safe, Adam was beginning to wonder if they were on a wild goose chase.

That's when, out of the corner of his eye, Adam noticed a moving box behind a dumpster. It seemed out of place, like someone had placed it there on purpose when it could have easily fit in the dumpster. This sent up a red flag to Adam, causing him to lead Valor over to the area. It was clear within a few minutes that Valor definitely smelled something that was triggering him to examine it further. As his sniffing and snorting sped up and his tail went crazy,

Adam knew they had found an explosive device. Valor sat down next to it, prompting Adam to raise his hand with a closed fist, the signal that the Woody cop needed to go inform the detonation team that they had found a bomb.

An hour later, their explosive device had been safely detonated and the area had been cleared, finding only one other explosive device in the neighborhood. Once they were sure there weren't anymore, the DCSRA team loaded back up into their trucks.

"Good work, team. I know it's in bad form to brag, but I have to commend you on your expert work today. Our team found both of the bombs, to the Dallas bomb squad's chagrin. Just goes to prove, DCSRA really does train the best of the best. Mother and Father are proud of you."

"I told you not to worry; when it came down to it, you'd be able to execute a search without a problem," Clara leaned over and whispered. "Miller's right. I am proud of the entire team, but what he doesn't know is how hard this was for you. You were in a high stress, possibly anxiety-triggering situation, and you didn't flinch. Excellent job, Adam."

A satisfied smile formed on Adam's face. He knew he had done well today, but Clara's high praise made his heart fill with pride. He wasn't sure when it became so important, but he reveled in her approval. He slowly moved his hand over on the bench, closing the few inches between them. With no one watching, his fingers grabbed the side of her hand and squeezed. She turned the palm of her hand up and squeezed back. It was a small gesture, but it meant the world to Adam.

As they returned to the DCSRA, Adam basked in the pleasure of a job well done, and the secret affection of the woman he cared deeply about.

## TWELVE

The rest of the week passed with them preparing for the mock simulation. By the time the day arrived, Adam was certain he was going to make Clara proud.

The team stood outside the urban rubble training grounds that had been set with various props, decoys, and live victims. None of the teams had been given previous access, making it fair for all of them.

The captain came to the front of the forty-two trainees that still remained. "Good afternoon, DCSRA trainees. Today marks the end of your training with us. We're confident that all of you will prove yourselves worthy of being called Disaster City Search and Rescue Academy graduates. Each of you represent the best of the best in the search and rescue world. On this final day, each of you get to demonstrate the skills you've mastered during two hundred hours of the most intense, most elite S & R training in existence. When you exit these grounds, remember, you represent the most prestigious academy in the world. Go make us proud."

The captain stepped back letting the teams move forward onto the training grounds. Adam was shocked at the level of detail present. There were two police cars, an ambulance, and a fire truck set up around the area. There were off-duty members from neighboring departments of each, already moving around as if in a real-life scenario.

Adam glanced around and noticed that the other teams seemed to be taking in the surroundings. His instinct told him he was wasting time, so without further thought, he gave Valor the cue to start searching. They worked their way through the rubble on the west end of the training grounds. Valor found a few decoys but didn't make the mistake of falling for them. They bypassed them and continued on. Further into the rubble, he heard groaning and realized there was a victim nearby. He knew it wasn't in the scope of his job to find victims, but they were supposed to be working together as a team. He moved closer to find a woman half-buried between two pieces of wood. Adam raised his hand to gesture over to one of the nearby rescue teams. He pointed out the victim, then moved on to search for any signs of an actual explosive device.

Thirty minutes passed and all Adam and Valor had to show for their time was two more decoys they managed to avoid. He was beginning to wonder if there were any bombs planted in the area at all. Just as he was about to give up and switch sections, Valor's tail started to wag in the pattern that indicated he smelled something. His interest was being drawn to a corner of a nearby building. Adam let Valor guide him over to the spot, and he noticed that he was homed in on a drain pipe. Valor moved closer, his inspection becoming more intense every second. By the time he sat down next to it, Adam knew there was a bomb in the pipe. He raised his hand to signal he'd found an explosive device.

Once it was confirmed, his first successful location set off a ripple effect. After that, they found three more bombs as well as another victim. By the end of the mock scenario, Adam was certain he had succeeded in being one of the best performers of the day.

The scenario concluded, and the trainees, civilian volunteers, and DCSRA staff gathered in the middle to go over the results. Adam watched as Clara, along with the other instructors, came to stand at the front of the group with the captain and Sarge in the center.

"I'm sorry, I'm late," one of the male civilians said, rushing up to the group. "I didn't know the event ended."

The man must have tripped on something, stumbling forward and knocking straight into Clara who was standing at the edge of the group. They both went tumbling towards the ground. There was the familiar popping sound that the devices made when they were triggered. Normally it wouldn't be a problem, but Clara wasn't wearing protective gear since she hadn't been in the scenario.

Adam darted forward, pushing people out of his way so he could get to Clara. She must have borne most of the blast because she was covered in bright green paint. He stooped down beside her, asking frantically, "Are you okay? Can you see all right?"

Clara rolled over and blinked several times. She brushed her hair out of her face, which had come loose from her bun. "I'm fine, just a little banged up."

"Thank goodness. I was so worried when I thought you might be hurt. I didn't know what I would do." Without thinking of the consequences, he bent forward and placed a kiss on her lips.

There were several gasps, along with grumbles from the growing crowd, but in that moment, Adam didn't care. He simply needed to kiss the woman he was falling for.

## THIRTEEN

The aftermath from her public kiss with Adam had been more intense than Clara would've ever suspected. She received a lengthy lecture by her superiors that it was unprofessional to allow a romantic relationship to develop with a trainee. They decided that due to her glowing record up until that point though, they wouldn't fire her over it. She would, however, be receiving a letter of formal reprimand in her file.

They weren't the only ones who were upset with her though. Ever since the incident, she received disapproving looks from her fellow instructors and almost all of the trainees. It seemed they all thought that because of how she felt about Adam, she had been giving him special treatment. She wasn't sure how to convince them that wasn't the case.

The day of graduation came, and Clara wasn't sure how she felt about it. Part of her was glad to get this class behind her, but the other part knew that meant Adam would be returning to his life in the Army. She'd been stupid enough to get caught up in her feelings for him. She never completely considered the fact she might jeopardize her reputation over something that was never meant to last.

Clara sat with the other instructors behind the captain, who was standing behind the podium in the amphitheater.

"I have to say, I'm rather impressed with the lot of you," the captain praised with a proud grin. "I wasn't sure what to expect with so many issues that occurred with this class. We had nearly half our initial recruits leave due to training accidents or an inability to keep up with the requirements. Even with your limited numbers, however, you've far exceeded many classes before you. Today, as we give each of you a pin of completion, know that it means you have proven yourself worthy. Wear it with pride, knowing that you are the best of the best."

The trainees came up one at a time, receiving

their certificate along with their pin. They turned to face the cameras, each taking a photo with first the captain, then the sergeant. Adam was towards the last of the names to be called. The captain had thought about withholding his top honors ribbon, but after talking with Miller who confirmed all of Adam's accomplishments, they decided to award it to him anyway.

As he came forward, Clara couldn't help but watch him with pride. She had to mask how proud she was of him, of course, since they both had steered clear of each other since the public kiss. Today, though, she could watch him, along with everyone else, and not be judged for it. Despite the fact that she had a blemish on her record because of him, she was glad that he was going to finally be able to get the assignment he always wanted. She cared about Adam and wanted him to succeed.

There was a small reception after the graduation. Everyone was more relaxed now that there was no longer the instructors and trainee division. All of them were simply DCSRA graduates.

Adam came up and pulled Clara to the side. "I need to talk with you about what happened."

"There's nothing to discuss," she whispered,

glancing around to make sure no one could hear them. "I shouldn't be talking with you, Adam."

"I know that I made a mistake when I kissed you publicly like that. It was stupid and impulsive, and I should have thought about what would happen to you because of it."

"It wasn't just a mistake because it was public. It shouldn't have happened at all. It was a mistake to get involved with you in the first place. I knew better, but I let my attraction to you override my good judgment. Now, I have to bear the consequences for my actions."

"I know you want to pretend that what's between us is merely attraction. It would make it easier to dismiss it, but we both know it's more than that. I care about you, Clara."

"Well, you shouldn't. We have different lives. You're going to get a new assignment overseas. I'm going to have a new batch of recruits coming in. It will never work between us."

"You don't know that," Adam argued. "If you would just consider giving us a chance."

Clara shook her head. "There's no point. It's better to just move on."

"I can't believe you mean that. I won't."

Clara could see the hurt in Adam's eyes. She

wished she hadn't put it there, but if she had to hurt him to let go of what he thought they could be, she would do it. "Your time here is done, Adam, which means we are done. Besides, once you get back to your life in the Army, I'll become a distant memory of a nice time you had while at training. Look, I have to go, but have a safe trip back to Colorado."

Clara turned around and left before she changed her mind. If she stayed one more minute around him, she was afraid she might let him kiss her again. That wasn't going to happen though. It was time for both of them to move on.

## FOURTEEN

Two weeks had passed since Adam had returned to his Army base in Clear Mountain. Though he enjoyed returning to his church and friends, he couldn't keep from thinking about Clara and what he'd left behind.

"Adam, did you hear me?" Aiden asked, a puzzled look on his face. "I asked you three times what toppings you want on the pizza."

"I'm good with whatever," he mumbled out, realizing he had been distracted with thoughts of Clara again.

"Geez, ever since you got back from your training, you've been acting really weird. What happened to you in Texas?"

Adam hadn't discussed it with anyone, thinking that with time, he would stop caring about Clara and it wouldn't matter. That hadn't been the case. Instead, he found himself thinking about her more and more. If not talking about it wasn't working, he wondered if he did discuss it with someone, it could help him move on.

"I met someone," Adam admitted. "But before you ask, it was doomed from the start."

"Why is that?" Aiden probed. "Often we think that's the case, but there's usually a solution to any problem."

"Not this time, Aiden. This time, I fell for the wrong woman."

"If you like her, she can't be. Why don't you bring her over sometime so we can meet her?"

Adam shook his head. "That's not going to happen. She was my instructor at the academy."

"Oh, I see," Aiden said, closing his laptop and coming to sit down by his friend. "Pizza can wait. This I need to hear. Tell me everything."

Adam spent the next twenty minutes telling Aiden all about Clara and what happened between them.

"Look, I can't tell you what to do. All I can do is point you in the direction of where I get my answers. Pray about it, Adam. God will show you what to do."

The advice was solid. Adam had been trying to figure all of this out on his own, when really, he should have been asking for God's help. Later that evening, he spent an hour in prayer, and by the end of it, he knew what he needed to do. He picked up his cell phone and dialed Clara's phone number. She answered on the second ring.

"Why are you calling me, Adam?"

He could hear the exasperation in her voice, but he didn't let it deter him. "I had to call you, Clara. I can't stop thinking about you. I know you're going to say it will pass, but I don't think so. It's been the exact opposite. The longer I'm away from you, the more intense my feelings grow."

"It still doesn't change anything about our situation."

"You're right; it doesn't. I also don't think you were willing to listen to me when I was there at Disaster City. I'm hoping you will now. I think we should try to make a long-distance relationship work."

"That's just it, Adam, they don't work. I've known too many people that have fallen into that trap. We'll agree to try. We'll call each other, video chat, and even make a couple of trips back and forth. Eventually, it will become too much though, and we'll call it quits. Meanwhile, our feelings will deepen, and the breakup will be ten times worse. This way, we cut our losses before we let our hearts get involved."

"My heart is already involved," Adam lamented. "Cutting me off hasn't stopped that from happening."

There were some voices drifting in from Clara's phone. "Look, I have to go, Adam. It's sweet that you want to make this work, but I just don't see any way it can."

He heard the click from her end, and the silence hit him like a ton of bricks. He had envisioned the phone call going so differently in his head. He thought she cared about him as much as he did her. Now, he wondered if he had been mistaken.

As he placed his cell phone back in his pocket, a deep sadness took hold of his heart. He wondered how he was ever going to get over Clara.

## FIFTEEN

The news that the captain was retiring and that Sarge was taking over the running of the academy had come as a shock to everyone. With the vacancy of a second in command, several of the instructors put in for the position. To Clara's surprise, Miller was chosen to take the job, leaving her firmly without someone to run the bomb detection classes with.

"What are we going to do, boy?" Clara asked, rubbing the top of Rebel's head. "I hate the idea of replacing Miller with some random stranger."

Letting out a heavy sigh, she stood up and made her way over to the computer. She decided to catch up on her emails and look at the list of new recruits coming at the beginning of next month.

The third email down contained pictures from the last class. She clicked the button and scrolled through it. Picture after picture, Adam's handsome face kept showing up. Her hand faltered as she saw one in which she was talking to him. It had been during the first week, but even at that point, it was clear there was something between them.

Even though she had tried to forget about Adam over the past month, her heart wouldn't let her. She had told him that a long-distance relationship wasn't worth trying. Unfortunately, she had found herself contemplating multiple times whether she should call him back and tell him she was willing to take the risk.

Had she been stupid to give up on the potential they had? Did she let a good guy pass her by because she was afraid of getting hurt? If she had, was there a way to fix it now?

Then an idea came to her. She needed a partner to help her teach at the academy. Adam had graduated at the top of his class. He was one of the best handlers she'd ever seen, and he would be a real asset to the academy.

Clara set to work on her plan. It would take a lot of favors, and she would have to pull some major strings, but she was going to do whatever it took to set things right.

## SIXTEEN

The phone rang and Adam glanced down at the screen. Clara's name flashed across it. Should he answer it? Last time they talked, she'd made it pretty clear that she wasn't interested in anything with him, but here she was calling him. Did that mean she'd changed her mind?

Knowing he couldn't live with himself if he didn't find out, he answered the call. "Hello."

"Hey, Adam, I was hoping you might have a few minutes to talk."

"What's going on, Clara?"

"I have some news."

"What kind of news?" Adam asked with apprehension. He didn't like surprises.

"The captain decided to retire and Sarge is taking over the academy."

"Is that so? The captain was great, but Sarge will do a good job. I'm not really sure why you're calling to tell me this though."

"Because Miller will be second in command. With him moving up to an administrative position, it leaves a spot open in the bomb detection unit."

"Still not sure why you're calling me," Adam said, the irritation clear in his voice. "This is the kind of stuff you tell your boyfriend, Clara, and you made it clear you didn't want that to be me."

"That's where you're wrong, Adam. I did want that, but I didn't see how it could ever work between us. That's when I realized this was the perfect solution. You need to take the position in the bomb detection unit."

"Wait, what?" he stammered out in confusion. "How would that even work? I still have two years left on my Army contract."

"I know that, and before I even called you to offer you the job, I checked with everyone involved. The captain is ex-Army—I'm not sure if you knew that—and as a parting gift to me, he called in a favor. If you want the position at DCSRA, he got them to agree to allow you to finish out your contract here where you can train Army recruits in detection."

"You did that?"

"Yes, I want us to work, Adam, and that means we have to be together. I know it was your dream to work overseas in hot zones, but you can still do a lot of good by training other officers and soldiers to do what you do. Think of how many people they could save? That could be the legacy you leave behind, and the way you honor your squad."

"I don't know what to say."

"I'm hoping you'll say yes. If you do, the next class starts in a week. You'd have to be here by then."

Adam wasn't sure what to say. He felt like he was in shock from the offer, but when he thought about it, all that mattered was finding a way to be with Clara.

"Do you need time to consider your options? I can understand if you need to. It's a big decision, and it means giving up your original plan for a new one."

"You're right, but I don't need time. Being with you is what I want most in this world, Clara. I'm all in. I'll take the job."

Clara's voice was filled with joy. "Really? You don't know how happy I am to hear that."

"Good, because I want to spend the rest of our lives making this new plan the best one ever."

EPILOGUE

Three months later

Adam was settled into his new home at the academy. It was the final week of his third class, and he'd finally found his rhythm of being an instructor. Clara helped a lot with it. She was great at helping him when he stumbled over what to do or say.

The first time Miller visited his class with its set of new recruits, he told him he did a good job. His only suggestion was to start using the Mother/Father terms on them, citing it would work perfectly since Adam and Clara were actually together in real life.

Deciding it put a little too much pressure on their relationship at the stage they were in, Adam had quietly declined using the names for him and Clara. Once they got married and had their first kid though, he might reconsider it.

There was a small knock on his apartment door, and he opened it to find Clara on the other side.

"It's good to see you," he said before leaning forward to give her a kiss.

"What are you up to?" Clara said, coming in and taking a seat on the couch.

"Just going over the list of potential DCSRA recruits for our next class," he explained as he took a seat on the couch next to her. He picked up his laptop and started going through the list again. "It still boggles my mind that out of hundreds of applicants, we only take six."

"We only train the best of the best," Clara pointed out. "That means we have to pick and choose who we let in."

"It really makes me appreciate the fact I got in, particularly when I look at all these incredible candidates."

"That's the hardest part, deciding who's worthy

of getting a spot." She leaned over and looked at the list. "Anyone that stands out?"

Halfway down the list, a familiar name jumped out at Adam. "As a matter-of-fact, there is, but his application must have gotten placed on our list by mistake. I know him from when I lived in Clear Mountain. Ted Hendricks is a top-notch search and rescue officer and works in all sorts of terrain. He's wanted to work as a K9 handler since I first met him, but they only have two on the team in Clear Mountain. He's applying for the open position in the specialized terrain division. It has a dog listed here as his partner, so I'm not sure how he managed that."

"Well, I think you should walk over to the staff office and personally tell them about your friend. A personal recommendation from one of our best new hires will make all the difference in him getting the position."

"You really think so?"

She nodded. "He'll be a shoo-in."

"It would be great to have a friend around the place. He's a good guy."

"That might be true, but don't forget, instructors don't fraternize with trainees."

"Sometimes the rules have to be broken. After

all, that's how we ended up together."

"I guess you're right; it's about time things were shaken up around here anyway."

"Didn't we do that enough?" Adam teased.

"Hey, can I help it that I fell victim to your charms? It's not every day that a handsome Army sergeant sweeps me off my feet."

"Is that what I did?"

She nodded. "I just didn't want to admit it."

"Well, now that you have—finally—it means I can do this whenever I want," he said, leaning over and kissing her again. "I rather like that."

She shook her head. "You can do it anywhere besides in front of the children."

"Children?" Adam asked with a quirk of his eyebrows.

"Yes, I think Miller's right. We need to be Mother and Father from now on. It's tradition after all."

"All right, if you insist."

"Don't sound so happy about it," she mocked, giving him a small playful punch in the arm.

"I am happy, you know. You make me happy. It's why I'll give in to anything you want."

"Good, that makes it easy for me. All I want is you."

This time, Adam pulled her towards him, wanting to feel her close. He let his lips move to meet hers, and the kiss was like having a piece of heaven come down to greet him. He knew in that moment he was exactly where he was supposed to be.

# A NOTE FROM THE AUTHOR

I hope you have enjoyed my final contemporary Lawkeeper book, *Lawfully Heroic*, and plan to read the rest of the Lawkeeper series written by me and several other amazing authors. You can read any and all of my Clear Mountain Lawkeeper romances to find out how Aiden, Zach, Connor, and Liam all found love. Don't worry, this isn't the end though for me writing about lawmen. Ted's story will continue in the very first Disaster City Search and Rescue book, *The Girlfriend Rescue*. There's also four other best selling authors writing in this brand new epic, adventure-filled, romance series. You can find out more about that on the next page.

Your opinion and support matters, so I would greatly appreciate you taking the time to leave a review. If you would like more info, please join my Newsletter and get a free novella just for signing up. I'd also love for you to check out My Reader's Group!

Happy Reading!

Jenna Brandt

## DISASTER CITY SEARCH AND RESCUE

Step into the world of Disaster City Search and Rescue, where officers, firefighters, military, and medics, train and work alongside each other with the dogs they love, to do the most dangerous job of all — help lost and injured victims find their way home.

The Girlfriend Rescue

The Mountain Rescue

The Whirlwind Rescue

The Plus One Rescue

The Reject Rescue

ALSO BY JENNA BRANDT

**Most Books are Free in Kindle Unlimited too!**

**The Lawkeepers** is a multi-author series alternating between historical westerns and contemporary westerns featuring law enforcement heroes that span multiple agencies and generations. Join bestselling author Jenna Brandt and many others as they weave captivating, sweet and inspirational stories of romance and suspense between the lawkeepers — and the women who love them. The Lawkeepers is a world like no other; a world where lawkeepers and heroes are honored with unforgettable stories, characters, and love. Jenna's Lawkeeper books:

**Historical**

Lawfully Loved-Texas Sheriff

Lawfully Wanted-Bounty Hunter

Lawfully Forgiven-Texas Ranger

Lawfully Avenged-US Marshal

Lawfully Covert-Spies

Lawfully Historical Box Set

## Contemporary

Lawfully Adored-K-9

Lawfully Wedded-K-9

Lawfully Treasured-SWAT

Lawfully Dashing-Female Cop/Christmas

Lawfully Devoted-Billionaire Bodyguard/K-9

Lawfully Heroic-Military Police

Lawfully Contemporary Box Set

## Disaster City Search and Rescue

Step into the world of Disaster City Search and Rescue, where officers, firefighters, military, and medics, train and work alongside each other with the dogs they love, to do the most dangerous job of all — help lost and injured victims find their way home.

The Girlfriend Rescue

The Wedding Rescue

The Billionaire Rescue

The Movie Star Rescue

## Billionaires of Manhattan Series

The billionaires that live in Manhattan and the women who love them. If you love epic dates, grand romantic gestures, and men in suits with hearts of gold, then these are books are perfect for you.

[Waiting on the Billionaire](underline)

[(Also on Audiobook)](underline)

[Nanny for the Billionaire](underline)

[Merging with the Billionaire](underline)

## Second Chance Islands

What's better than billionaires on islands? How about billionaires finding second chances at life, love, and redemption while on one.

[The Billionaire's Reunion](underline)

[The Billionaire's Hideaway](underline)

## Billionaire's Birthday Club

Billionaire Birthday Club is an exclusive resort—for the billionaire who appears to have everything but secretly wants more. After filling out a confidential survey, a curated celebration is waiting on the island to make their birthday wishes come true!

[The Billionaire's Birthday Wish](underline)

## Holliday Islands Resort

After growing his Alaskan resort empire into the

"honeymooner's paradise of the world," Gordon Holliday is ready to retire. But there's no way he can cruise the globe in his luxury yacht until his sons are groomed and polished into proper executives to take his place. There's just one catch: He's convinced their biggest current job requirement is marriage!

<u>Comet's Blazing Love</u>

**Match Made in Heaven Series**-standalone stories that are sweet, clean romances designed to whisk you away. Not every man has six-pack abs, nor every woman the model of femininity, but everyone needs someone. We believe in building a world that begins at the very core of what makes romance stories work—faith, hope, and love. Now it's your turn to find love. Set your imagination and heart free with us. The next happily-ever-after is at your fingertips, just waiting to be told… Jenna's Matched books:

<u>Royally Matched-Contemporary</u>

<u>Discreetly Matched-Historical</u>

**Pinkerton Matchmaker Series**

As female agents were few and far between, Mr. Gordon came up with the idea of expanding the detective agency by pairing qualified women with a male agent for training, guidance and undercover work. These women came from all demographics – some were looking for a new life, some seeking challenge, some wanting to pave the way for future generations of women. The only caveat – the women wouldn't be a member of the Agency until their first assignment had been completed.

## An Agent for Nadine

## An Agent for Gwendolyn

**Mail Order Mistakes Series**-a mail order bride story about a woman running from a broken past and a widower with three children who is hiding from a broken heart. What happens when they decide to take a chance on each other?

Mail Order Misfit

Mail Order Misstep (coming soon)

Mail Order Miscast (coming soon)

## The Civil War Brides Series

During the bloodiest conflict on American soil, two families struggle in the South to not only survive but to thrive.

Saved by Faith

Freed by Hope

Healed by Grace (Early 2020)

**Silverpines Series**-centered around the fictional town of Silverpines, Oregon, during the turn of the 20th century. When a disaster takes most of the men, the women are left to save the town by placing mail-order grooms advertisements. Get to know the various lovable characters and their stories from some of todays bestselling historical authors.

<u>Wanted: Tycoon</u>

<u>The Tycoon's Sister</u>

**Bride Herder Series**-take one failed rancher turned matchmaker and ten unexpected brides at once with no clue as to who wanted them. What could go wrong?

<u>Herd to Please</u>

**Belles of Wyoming Series**-centered around the fictional small town of Belle, Wyoming. Each set of books take place during a season of the year in the 1800s.

<u>June's Remedy</u>

**The Window to the Heart Saga** is a recountal of the epic journey of Lady Margaret, a young English noblewoman, who through many trials, obstacles, and tragedies, discovers her own inner strength, the sustaining force of faith in God, and the power of family and friends. In this three-part series, experience new places and cultures as the heroine travels from England to France and completes her adventures in America. The series has compelling themes of love, loss, faith and hope with an exceptionally gratifying conclusion.

Trilogy

The English Proposal (Book 1)

The French Encounter (Book 2)

The American Conquest (Book 3)

Spin-offs

The Oregon Pursuit (Book 1)

The White Wedding (Book 2)

The Christmas Bride (Book 3)

The Viscount's Wife (Book 4)

The Window to the Heart Saga
Trilogy Box Set

The Window to the Heart Saga
Spin-off Books Box Set

The Window to the Heart Saga

Complete Collection Box Set

For more information about Jenna Brandt visit her on any of her websites.

www.JennaBrandt.com

Jenna Brandt's Reader Group

www.facebook.com/JennaBrandtAuthor

www.twitter.com/JennaDBrandt

Signup for Jenna Brandt's Newsletter

# JOIN MY MAILING LIST AND READER'S GROUP

**Sign-up for my newsletter and get a FREE story.**

**Join my Reader Group and get access to exclusive content and contests.**

## ACKNOWLEDGMENTS

My writing journey would not be possible without those who supported me. Since I can remember, writing is the only thing I love to do, and my deepest desire is to share my talent with others.

First and foremost, I am eternally grateful to Jesus, my lord and savior, who created me with this "writing bug" DNA.

In addition, many thanks go to:

My husband, Dustin, and three daughters, Katie, Julie, and Nikki, for loving me and supporting me during all my late-night writing marathons and coffee-infused mornings.

My mother, Connie, for being my first and most honest critic, now and always. As a little girl, sleeping under your desk during late-night deadlines for the local paper showed me what being a dedicated writer looked like.

My angels in heaven: my grandmother, who passed away in 2001; my infant son, Dylan, who was taken by SIDS five years ago; and my father, who left us three years ago

To my ARC Angels for taking the time to read my story and give valuable feedback.

And lastly, but so important, to my dedicated readers, who have shared their love of my books with others, helping to spread the words about my stories. Your devotion means a great deal.

## ABOUT THE AUTHOR

Jenna Brandt is an award-winning, international best selling, historical and contemporary romance author. Her historical books span from the Victorian to Western eras and all of her books have elements of romance, suspense and faith. Her debut series, the Window to the Heart Saga, as well as her Billionaires of Manhattan Series, have become best-selling series, and her multi-author series, The Lawkeepers, Silverpines, Belles of Wyoming, and Bride Herders are fan-favorites.

She has been an avid reader since she could hold a book and started writing stories almost as early. She has been published in several newspapers as well as edited for multiple papers. She graduated with her Bachelor of Arts in English from Bethany College and was the Editor-in-Chief of the newspaper while there. Her first blog was published on Yahoo Parenting and The Grief Toolbox as well as featured on the ABC News and Good Morning America websites.

Writing is her passion, but she also enjoys cooking, watching movies, reading, engaging in social media and spending time with her three young daughters and husband where they live in the Central Valley of California. She is also active in her local church where she volunteers on their first impressions team.

Made in United States
North Haven, CT
20 November 2023

44295962R00086